All of
Our Monsters

and other stories and poems

Rebecca Serim Lee

TABLE OF CONTENTS

SHORT STORIES

POEMS

SHORT STORIES

It was Claude's first day in the psychiatric hospital when her monster visited.

Her Aunt Amelie had just finished overseeing her registration into the ward, and was now preparing to leave. A nurse hastily set up a tray of food and water on Claude's bedside table while shooting furtive glances at Aunt Amelie. It was nothing new. While the posh lady brandished a pair of Bvlgari sunglasses and dusted imaginary lint off her leopard-print coat, everyone else stared.

The nurse turned to Claude. "My name is Celine," she spoke softly, gazing at Claude as if the girl were some fragile twig about to snap in half. "I'll be taking care of you during your stay."

It was all Claude could do to not scoff. As if her stay here were more like a vacation getaway than a form of torture. But she nodded politely and murmured, "Thank you, Celine."

Aunt Amelie, on the other hand, truly scoffed. "Don't worry, Celeste, the only thing she needs is a brain and some skin on her bones. That better be so when I come back to pick her up."

With that, she left, the tail of her faux coat swishing behind her. Claude could practically see her own reflection in her aunt's glossy blond hair. She imagined a frail, bony figure with dirty blond hair in ratty knots.

"I'm sorry about her," Claude murmured to her nurse. "People like her never change." And Claude, as she knew deep inside, was exactly like her.

"No need to worry." Celine smiled. "If you need anything, do not hesitate to press that button." She pointed to a small red circle on the side of Claude's bed, then scurried out.

Claude closed her eyes and leaned back in her bed. She suddenly felt so incredibly tired, and wanted nothing more than to sleep for a week. She must have dozed off, because when she opened her eyes again, a pretty girl was sitting on the chair by her window. She was staring at Claude intently.

There was no surprise beating in Claude's heart. "Who are you?"

The girl blinked her blue eyes, much like Claude's, and flipped her lustrous golden hair. "The real question is, who are *you*?"

Claude sat up. "I'm Claude. Now answer my question."

She didn't get any answers. The girl got out of her chair delicately, unfolding her dainty legs, and made her way to the mirror over the small sink. She leaned in to check her reflection, reapplying a lip tint to her plump lips. Her skin was so perfect, it nearly glowed, and her body was enough to make any man salivate. Claude pushed down the jealousy that grew in her stomach.

The girl sighed. "I'm so ugly, aren't I? I'm an absolute monster, that's what I am."

"But you're not," Claude blurted out. She must have been drugged with some kind of sleep medication, because she felt groggy and her mouth was loose. She said, "I wish I were like you."

The girl cocked her head, turning to Claude. "And what do you mean by that?" Something in her voice sounded like she already knew the answer.

Claude had been raised by her aunt, who was a very sophisticated woman. Her aunt was pushing her forties, but still got complimented on her looks. She was impossibly beautiful for her age, and never failed to revel in that fact. Growing up, Claude wanted to be like her, and her aunt wanted Claude to be like her as well. She was never allowed to eat candy, and every single meal was disgusting in how healthy it was. She could never play sports because she was too elegant. She went shopping every week for makeup and clothes. Claude had been competing in child beauty pageants for as long as she could remember. She was known by everyone as the little doll come to life.

But it, of course, eventually had its burden on Claude's bony shoulders. She felt pressured to watch every meal like a hawk, wear only the most fashionable clothes, and be the prettiest girl in Paris. Everything became a competition, especially her appearance. She weighed herself every night and compared with her friends. If a single pound was gained, she spent the next day fasting. The pattern became more severe as she grew up. Her body needed food for sustainment, but she refused to let her perfect face gain a single pinch of fat. Doctors soon diagnosed her with anorexia, and it disgusted her naturally-perfect aunt enough that she found the nearest psychiatrist hospital.

But Claude didn't say any of this to the girl. Instead, she said, "You're just perfect, and so very pretty. I wish I were like that. Who are you, though?"

The girl smiled. "Claude, you may think we are different people, but the truth is far from that. I am the prettiest version of yourself that you could ever be. I am both the image you hate most and the person you wish to become."

Claude frowned and looked closer. She could recognize parts of herself. Those blue eyes, blond hair, and the beauty mark dotting her cheek right next to her nose. Yes, indeed, it was herself. "How is that possible?"

"I am a monster. I take the form of your most hidden secrets and haunt you until you break. Your secret, Claude, is that you fear you will never become the person you most desire. You fear that someday, another girl will come along—one who is prettier than you—and take your throne. You fear that you won't ever be good enough, and that you will fail. That you will disappoint yourself, and your aunt, and everyone else who ever called you the prettiest girl alive."

It couldn't be denied. Now that her secrets had all been spoken aloud, Claude felt smaller than a mouse. She could see herself in the mirror, sitting on a bed and looking pitiful. Eyebags weighed down on her face, and her hair was a mess. In fact, her entire body was a mess. Her ribs poked through her skin and her skin was pallid. She looked at the girl, the monster, who was herself. It had sun-kissed skin, luminous eyes, silky hair, and the body of a goddess. Claude curled her fists until her nails broke the skin of her hands. She felt a surge of anger, so palpable that she swore the mirror cracked in response.

The monster smiled knowingly and turned back to the mirror. "Such fragile little things we are, aren't we? So vulnerable and easy to crack open. Just like this mirror here, in a way." Without warning, its hand flashed out and struck the mirror. It cracked, dropping a shard. The monster picked it up and walked over to the bed. Left above the sink was a broken reflection of Claude, webbed with cracks and nursing a gaping hole.

Claude had never hated herself more than in that moment. She just wished that she could be perfect like the girl—no, even more than that, she just wished everything would *stop*. She wished there was a way out of this hellhole, and she could find a world to live in where she wouldn't have to starve herself and check her reflection with every breath she took. She wished.

The monster offered the broken shard of glass to Claude. "You have a choice here. Press that button to fix the broken mirror—" it nodded to the red one Celine had pointed out earlier "—or you can take this shard of glass and scar yourself. You'll never be pretty again, at least not in the eyes of your aunt. You'll be marred permanently. But it'll be your way out of this, your sweet relief. You'll never live the life you know now."

Claude looked down at the shard, so tiny but sharp at the edges. The answer was simple, wasn't it? Some part of her, instinctive and rooted deep inside her from the beginning, knew what to do.

The monster asked, "So what'll it be?"

On the other side of the world, Phillip was standing on the roof of the Nashville General Hospital when his monster showed up.

He and his older brother Caleb had been in the car earlier that day when they got in a terrible accident. Next thing Phillip knew, he was herded into an ambulance with Caleb on a stretcher, and they were on their way to the ER. The siren shrieked throughout the ride, and Phillip sat there numbly looking down at his brother's bloodied body. By then, though, it was too late. Caleb was dead.

Phillip now stood on the edge of the hospital roof, staring at the sunset against the Nashville skyline. He had his phone in hand. The nurses made him promise to call his parents with the news, but Phillip had yet to carry out his oath. He contemplated throwing his phone down into the evening traffic.

"What'll it be, kid?"

Phillip turned around. He wasn't surprised to see Caleb, gory and grinning, staring at him and calling him nicknames like he always had. It didn't scare him when he started walking closer, bearing resemblance to a grisly zombie. Everything seemed natural.

"Who are you?" Phillip asked.

Caleb grinned wider. "Your very own monster. But what'll it be?"

"What'll what be?"

"Throw the phone down or call your parents. Jump off or back away."

"'Your,'" Phillip commented with a pause. "You said 'your parents', not ours. You're not really Caleb, aren't you?"

Not-Caleb grinned again, and took another step closer. "I'm not. I'm nothing but a figment of your imagination, coming to life in your greatest time of need. In fact, the only thing I am is *you*." Its face shifted for half a second, mirroring Phillip, but flashed back to Caleb just as fast. "I'm your deepest fears and flaws incarnate."

This didn't intimidate Phillip as much as it likely should have. He didn't feel anything but a strange sense of calm, for the first time in his life. Like he could float on his back in the ocean and let the current wash him away to paradise. "What are my deepest fears and flaws?"

Not-Caleb guffawed, and it sounded so much like Phillip's dead brother that a tear slipped down his cheek. "I thought you'd never ask! The problem is, chump—" it leaned in close "—you have no heart of your own. The only heart you ever allowed yourself to believe in stopped beating an hour ago. The only voice you ever listened to stopped speaking an hour ago. The only footsteps you ever followed stopped moving an hour ago."

Phillip bristled. "That's not true. And what is that even supposed to mean?"

He flinched as the monster suddenly swooped in close, a rank smell filling his nostrils, as they were practically nose-to-nose. It was then that Phillip could see the monster's eyes, burning an ominous red, and the blood steadily dribbling out of its open wounds. The blood seemed to run a little faster with each second that passed. The monster didn't say a single word, leaving Phillip's mind to fill in the cavities alone.

Phillip's parents never had a perfect marriage. Ever since he was a toddler, all he could remember was constant fighting. His father had a scar on his chin from when his mother threw a vase at him and a shard nicked his skin. His mother had a permanent limp from when his father pushed her down the stairs. Phillip had always been too terrified to say a word, and instead hid behind Caleb's back. Caleb was the one to lock them in his bedroom during every one of their parents' feuds. Caleb was the one to feed Phillip when the parents forgot about them. Once, during one of their physical fights, Caleb called the police. He went to school the next day with a black eye.

When their parents first started truly considering the option of divorce, Caleb began high school and joined the football team. He put all of his frustration from home into being an athlete, and in no time, he became a star. By his senior year, he was set to become a Division I athlete in college. Phillip, on the other hand, had no potential for athletics. He was skinny when Caleb was muscular. He was short when Caleb was tall. He had grown up following Caleb around like an obsessed fan, relying on him for safety and advice, and his idolization came to a point where he was willing to do anything Caleb did. After all, he had never known a different life. So, Phillip also joined the football team.

The day of the car crash was the day their parents had their court date regarding the divorce. Caleb had been behind the wheel, driving them towards the courthouse, when a car merging at the wrong time had pulled them into a head-on collision. Phillip was left with a broken arm. Caleb, of course, was left dead.

But now that Caleb was gone and Phillip was off the hook from playing football for a while, he wasn't sure what he was supposed to do. His parents probably hadn't even noticed that their sons failed to show up at court. Caleb was Phillip's best friend and his life support, and now Phillip was without either. He might as well be dead now that he had no purpose. That was the thought that propelled him to the hospital roof.

The monster's blood was now running much faster, spilling over its skin and down its body. It pooled at its feet and spread like poison, crawling towards Phillip. Phillip looked down at it impassively and then looked out at the sky. He felt his lips curling into a smile before his hand moved almost without him knowing, tossing the phone to the wind.

Not-Caleb smiled uncannily. "Your first decision has been made without the influence of someone else. Now you have one more. And you know already, deep down, what the answer will be. The only thing left is to do it."

Phillip walked towards the edge of the roof until his toes were almost in the air, almost levitating. Down below, headlights blurred together to create a glowing river of red. Behind him, blood raced down the monster's body, and the pool at its feet grew faster and faster. He could jump and follow Caleb, or he could walk away and find his own path without any guide to follow.

The monster asked, "So what'll it be?"

There is only one person in the world who has the ability of discovering what your monster is. That person is yourself.

Your monster, too, is yourself. We are the only ones who know what our deepest, most private insecurities are. It may be obsession over your appearance, or struggling to stand up for yourself, or something else completely. We are the only ones who know what kind of fears haunt our dreams, what kind of flaws wrinkle our palms. We are the ones who hide it from the rest of the world because we are too scared to put ourselves out in the open like that. We spend every passing second of the day trying to push it down, trying to sugarcoat it to make it seem like everything is okay. Our lives are filled with so many ups and downs that we can only forge one path ahead, and in doing so, fail to see the other solution: embrace your monster.

Your monster is part of what makes you the person you are. Too often when we think about ourselves, our minds turn to our flaws and bitterly wish they weren't true. Such is the case for myself, which is how I sit here today and tell you all this. But would that not make us all clones seeking to be perfect models of humanity? Being flawed is part of what makes us human— and yes, everyone has heard this mantra thousands of times before. But have we all realized it yet?

I have not yet discovered what my monster is. Yes, I am plagued by my own insecurities, ones that dictate every single move I make, every single breath I take. But my life hasn't been about trying to work through them. My life has been about trying to work around them, trying to avoid them in an attempt to make them any less haunting. Trying to forget about it because maybe that will make it all go away. There is no way of knowing how to change it, but we can all try. We can find our monsters, the incarnation of all our worst abominations, and find a way to cope with it. Or we can go on with our lives as they are, trying to become perfect, trying to be the very best version of ourselves, while valiantly attempting to ignore everything else.

So what'll it be?

Amelie was known as *Fille Graisse* from kindergarten through middle school. It meant Fat Girl, and people called her that because she was noticeably plump. Her doctors had warned her of morbid obesity if she continued to gain weight, but she couldn't help it—she loved eating.

At first, being called the Fat Girl didn't bother her that much. It all seemed like a game—people would call her *Fille Graisse*, and she'd laugh it off. But everything got worse in middle school. Bullies would write mean names all over her locker with red marker and spread rumors behind her back of what kind of things she ate for fun. When everyone's favorite neighborhood cat disappeared, Amelie was accused of having eaten it. They'd even gather around during lunchtime to see what kind of food she had.

It got to the point where Amelie refused to go to school. She stayed at home and starved herself. Her parents, who didn't mind her insatiable appetite, only worsened it by attempting to lighten her up with her favorite foods. Amelie's older sister Belle was the cheerleading captain at her high school and began overseeing how Amelie treated her body. She went back to school, but fasted for the next five months.

Eventually, she made a transformation so immense that hardly anybody could match her to her past appearance. They renamed her *Fille Petite*. Every girl in the grade started to worship her for her divine change, and for once in her life, boys didn't call her names but instead sought her attention. Amelie was desparate to keep her new status, and watched her diet very strictly. Belle only enforced her new behavior.

Her parents began to get concerned over how malnourished she was. By the time Amelie started high school, even the doctors were worried about how much change her body had undergone in such a short amount of time. For the first time, Amelie was told she was underweight. It made her ecstatic.

In tenth grade, Amelie's parents finally acted on her behaviour. When they learned Amelie had spent an entire week not eating, they sent her to the nearest psychological ward. There, they diagnosed her with anorexia. She was forced to receive treatment there for several months.

Amelie came back to school for eleventh grade, except she had gained thirty pounds from her stay in the hospital. Her change was noticed quickly, and rumors were immediately spread behind her back. The news of her diagnosis and time in the ward grew like wildfire. Belle treated her like a maid. Her status as *Fille Petite* was gone, replaced by *Fille Malade*. It meant Sick Girl.

Her life subsequently returned back to the way it had been during middle school—she lost all her friends and popularity, and was left to eat lunch alone in the cafeteria. She was forced to see a therapist on a regular basis, and her diet was no longer in her control. Amelie had lost the one thing that made her special—her slenderness.

Though her high school life never recovered, Amelie made her ultimate comeback in college. She cut off all ties with her family and moved across the country. Now that nobody was constantly keeping an eye on her body and diet, she restarted her lifestyle of fasting. She even got procedures to remove all marks from her skin, and to give her face a more slender appearance. She did everything in her power to have the "perfect body".

Her monster came to her on her day of college graduation. Amelie was standing in front of her vanity mirror, cinching her graduation gown this way and that to decide what would most flatter her body. Suddenly, a series of light knocks rapped on the door.

Sighing with scorn, Amelie walked over and opened it. She almost fell back onto her hind when she saw who was behind the door. "Belle?"

Belle walked in without further invitation, her nose held high. Yes, it was Belle—tall, slender, beautiful, and as arrogant as before. "What a disgusting little room. This is where you've been staying for the past four years?"

Amelie stumbled back towards the vanity mirror and sat down on the stool. She blinked at her older sister. Somehow, Belle was the same as the person she remembered, but also different. Everything she'd been before seemed to have doubled in degree.

Belle switched her disdainful gaze to Amelie's graduation gown. "Tsk. And how gross is that? If you're going to waste your time in college, at least graduate with some taste."

"I…" Amelie shook herself out of her stupor. "I was trying to find ways to fashion it, but… But what are you doing here? It's been four years!"

Her older sister waved a hand impatiently. "Yeah, yeah. You look great, by the way."

The comment struck Amelie. She felt a brief flutter. "Really?"

"At least, for someone who used surgeries to try and look beautiful, sure."

Amelie deflated. "How are Mama and Papa?"

"They said they miss back when you were home and they could feed you every night."

The nostalgia that had been growing in Amelie's chest disappeared. She sighed and was about to reach for her makeup kit when all of a sudden her phone rang. She picked it up and gasped at the name of the caller. It was her mother. With a trembling finger, Amelie answered the call.

"Mama—!"

Amelie was barely able to greet her mother for the first time in years when she was interrupted.

"I need you to look after Claude," panted her mother. "Just for tonight, maybe tomorrow night. Can you do it? Come home and pick her up."

Amelie froze. When she looked over at Belle, she was merely sitting on the bed and inspecting her perfectly groomed nails, a small smile on her face. Amelie turned and looked into the mirror. Had her face always been this gaunt? Had her hair always been this thin, her cheeks so sharp, her eyes so shallow?

"Who's Claude?" Amelie asked slowly.

For a few moments, all she could hear was the slight crackle of static as her mother didn't speak. Then, "Your niece. Did you not get the news? Belle had a child earlier this year. A daughter named Claude. You never contacted us so we weren't sure if you'd gotten the news."

Amelie was speechless. She looked over at Belle. Her older sister didn't seem to be showing any signs of postpartum. She looked as perfect as ever—better, even. "What happened?" she asked, mostly to herself than anyone else.

"Belle has gotten into a car accident," her mother panted. She sounded as if she was on the verge of tears. "They've taken her to the ER and aren't sure whether she'll make it. The doctors are saying she likely won't. Please, I'm begging you, just take your niece for tonight while we stay at the hospital."

"I will," Amelie said numbly. "I'll go as soon as I can." With that, she hung up.

When she spun around, Belle was no longer sitting on the bed. Amelie let out a gasp, then spotted her sister next to her, leaning into the vanity mirror. Without a warning, she yanked open Amelie's cosmetics drawers and fished out every single item her fingers could grasp. Amelie watched in horrified awe as Belle pulled open the eyebrow pen and drew a line straight between her two brows.

"What are you—"

Next was the lipstick. Belle scowled as she sifted through the different colors, then finally settled on an unflattering dark brown. With it, she drew an enormous circle around her mouth, nearly covering her nose and chin.

"Belle…" Amelie placed her hand on Belle's arm, then recoiled at what she felt. A thick layer of flesh surrounding her bone, flabby instead of thin.

Belle whipped around fiercely. Amelie hardly recognized her. "So what'll it be?" she asked mockingly, her lipstick-ravaged mouth twisted into a smirk.

Amelie was silent.

"Will you go play hero of the day," Belle continued, advancing a step, "or hide like a coward in your dank little dorm, living the life you worked so hard to build away from home?"

"Of course I'll go," Amelie said quietly. "She's your daughter."

"Not my daughter." Belle's smile grew. "Our niece."

Before Amelie had time to respond, Belle turned back to the cosmetics drawer. She pulled out an eyelid liner and uncapped it. Amelie cringed as she drew ugly black streaks from her forehead down to her neck.

"Do you believe in monsters?" Belle asked calmly. She looked like a nightmare.

"No."

"Well, you should." She took a cotton pad and smeared the inky streaks all over her face.

Amelie turned away, reaching for her car keys. She felt lightheaded; was she hallucinating? After all, she hadn't eaten an official meal in over a week. "I don't have time for this."

Belle sighed contentedly, gazing at the mirror. "Beauty. Such a strange thing, isn't it? The standards change by the day and you mortals, so desperate to fit in—or better, stand out as superior—are always too helpless to do anything. The things you do to be beautiful. Starvation; sabotage; self-neglect; malnourishment; does it ever end?"

Amelie grabbed her coat and slipped her arms into the sleeves. "Are you done yet?"

"Such a miserable life!" Belle didn't acknowledge Amelie. "Are you really content with letting your lives be controlled by something intangible, something that doesn't even have a conscience of its own?"

She suddenly snatched a half-empty water bottle nearby, discarded haplessly. Smiling widely, she poured the liquid all over her head. Makeup ran in rivulets down her face, leaving behind a canvas of ruined paints. Amelie had never seen a more horrific—nor a more magnificent—sight.

"Remember me, Amelie, when you make the final decision."

Amelie blinked, and the monster was gone.

Amelie stood on the porch of her parents' house, shivering from nerves, and rang the doorbell. She gazed down at the doormat. It was still the same as it had been from her earlier years; nothing was different.

The door suddenly swung open, and Amelie was greeted by the sight of her mother. She looked terrible. Not only had age weighed down unflatteringly on her entire face, but her skin was blotchy, eyes swollen. She was obviously grieving for the daughter she had not yet lost.

"Mama," Amelie said slowly. She hesitantly leaned in for a hug, then spotted a young child in the foyer.

Her mother followed her gaze and beckoned to the child. It was a girl, and she appeared to be almost a year old. "Claude, come."

Amelie stared at her niece. Claude looked exactly like her mother—yes, that was her golden blond hair, lustrous even in her infant years, and those blue doe-eyes, those pink lips and apple cheeks. Amelie almost laughed out of sheer disbelief.

Her father suddenly ran into the foyer behind Claude. He looked as rumpled as her mother. Without sparing time to greet his daughter, he said, "We must go to the hospital right away. Amelie, can you take Claude now?"

"Of course," Amelie said numbly. She awkwardly took her niece's hand. She wondered if she was also allowed to visit Belle, but kept her mouth closed.

As she walked Claude back to the car, she glanced up. Belle—at least the monstrous version of her—was standing across the street. Amelie nearly stumbled, but didn't trip. Belle was still drenched in water, her face running with hideous makeup, her mouth contorted in disdain. She watched silently as Amelie seated Claude in the child's seat she'd gotten from the nearest market as a last-minute emergency.

Amelie climbed into the driver's side, fastened her seatbelt, and turned the engine on. Just as she was about to pull out of the driveway, she looked up at the rearview mirror. Belle was still there, scowling with disapproval. Amelie watched as a car passed down the road, leaving an empty street in its wake.

THE JOURNEY OF MRS. HUR

In 1947, a woman was nearly shot by Soviet Union soldiers.

She, along with a group of fugitives, was walking through a field of frozen wheat when it happened. In the distance, soldiers were heard patrolling the night shift, armed with guns and brute strength. The woman, Mrs. Hur, crouched and hid with the other fugitives. She pressed her ten-month-old daughter to her chest. If a single sound was made, the entire group would have been shot to death—but luckily the infant kept quiet.

This woman is my great-grandparent, the mother of my mother of my mother. She was born in North Korea before fleeing to the south in the 1940s. Accompanying her were her cousin-in-law and her brother-in-law, both barely adults. They spent days trekking through the harsh, often mountainous, winter terrain in order to reach safety in the south.

Generations have set me and my great-grandmother so far apart that I am barely able to comprehend what her life was like. But I do know a bit about who she once was. She was a prim lady, born into a middle-class family. She was a proper woman with a proper job as a banker before her life fell apart. She was the kind of woman to always serve food on a tray, complete with neatly-arranged silver utensils and a stack of napkins. She was the kind of woman who never let her husband see her face without makeup on it. She was the kind of woman who dedicated her life to cooking and taking care of the house. She was the kind of woman who raised children of her own to inherit her proper manners. With all this in mind, I cannot begin to imagine what it must have been like for a lady like her to endure such a demanding journey.

The group of fugitives left in January of 1947, with the help of a paid guide. The man assisted them with navigating through the lands. They walked all night, when temperatures plummeted and everything was dark, and hid from the sun during the day. Some places were especially brutal—snow had piled up to their waists, and they waded laboriously through it, with Mrs. Hur holding her baby up high. Other than to nurse the child, which was difficult with snot blocking her little nose, they never once stopped to change clothes or rest. Mrs. Hur's toes got pulled out over time.

I am struck by the sheer difference of how the women of each generation have suffered. My great-grandmother's struggles were based on times of life or death, during a period of war, while mine are trivial and mundane in comparison. A frostbitten limb or severe malnourishment for her, and a mosquito bite and a growling stomach for me.

A teacher once told me that three generations cycle over and over in a family tree: the first is the most hardworking, humble generation; the second is less hardworking; and the third is not at all hardworking, but rather spoiled and lazy. If my great-grandmother falls into the first generation, then does the cycle repeat to deem me as her successor? This question haunts me all the time.

One night, the man who had been paid to guide the fugitives disappeared. He was nowhere to be seen. This left everyone with no one to rely on in order to make it south safely, and they resorted to navigating with the stars. Every night, they looked up at the dark sky and followed the constellations. They could only pray that the stars were leading them in the right direction.

What was left of Mrs. Hur's possessions was a lone golden ring hanging around her neck on a thread, and scarce money earned from selling her belongings. The money was tucked into the folds of her baby's clothes. Everything else had been left at home. Mrs. Hur and her family had been comfortable enough living in the north, but that changed once chaos bloomed. They abandoned all that they owned to seek a better future in the south.

The discord in the Korean peninsula all started with the end of Japanese control in 1945, once WWII ended. Korea was liberated, and thus a free land was left for occupation. The Soviet Union established control in the northern region, while the United States set up troops in the south. This introduced into the Korean population both communism and democracy respectively, sparking arguments between different people and marking the start of a time of violence.

The husband of Mrs. Hur was named Mr. Kim, and he studied Western Law in a Japanese university in Tokyo before the liberation. He came back home to the north, only to be greeted by communists targeting people of high wealth or education. This left Mr. Kim with no choice but to flee to the south, where democracy prevailed. Mrs. Hur stayed at home with her newborn, who was too young to travel at the time. She left once her daughter—my grandmother—was old enough. At this time, Mrs. Hur was only 22 years of age, and Mr. Kim was 24.

As one living a privileged life, I know what my life will be like when I'm 22. I am a girl raised by people of high intelligence and high standards. I will graduate from high school with flying colors, then get into a top-tier university ranked amongst the best in the nation. I will spend four years studying a major that will lead me to a well-paying job. At 22, I will graduate with a good GPA. Then I will transition into my life as a full-time working adult. My life, in a way, has already been planned out before I was even born, in the recesses of my parents' dreams.

Mrs. Hur's life had never been planned out, nor did she ever really get a chance to carve her own story until after she settled in Seoul. Will I ever face an unexpected, long path up a mountain like she had to? Will I have the strength to find the way back down like she did?

Finally, after a month of frightfully searching for and avoiding all signs of the soldiers' olive-green uniforms, the group reached the line of 38 degrees latitude, at which the peninsula was divided. The sounds of nature—of the birds, of the breeze rustling bare branches—all suddenly seemed miraculous to Mrs. Hur, even after days spent listening to them for warnings of danger. She walked to the nearest station, where she could find a train to ride into Seoul.

They finally reached the city—my great-grandmother, her baby, the two young men, and everyone else who had joined along the way—and it was like they had stepped into a completely new world. People of all kinds were walking around carefree, abuzz and lively, lacking a single worry of death waiting for them around the corner. One woman was even selling street foods at the side of the road, her voice carrying out over the crowds unimpeded. It was enough to make Mrs. Hur burst into tears as she rediscovered what life should have been like all along. She was in a new place, with a young baby to take care of and hardly any money, and yet she felt hope for the first time in ages.

Mrs. Hur would end up spending more than seven decades living in Seoul. What was initially a strange world became the place she would call home. Her two children would also grow up to call Seoul their home, as would their own children. My generation interrupts the tradition. After many prosperous years of a quiet life in Seoul, my generation has not been raised in Korea. We are all dominated by American nationality, and though Seoul heritage runs in our blood, it is not in our hands and mouth. We do not act nor speak like we are Korean. Mrs. Hur lived in Seoul until her recent death, but did not get to experience the fourth generation carry on her legacy in the city she helped rebuild. Instead, we are halfway across the world, where even her eagle eyes can't see us.

After her arrival in Seoul, Mrs. Hur reunited with Mr. Kim. They settled down peacefully for a couple years, having their second child, before the Korean War broke out in 1950. This forced them and many others to flee further south. Had Mrs. Hur escaped from the north later, she would not have been able to find her husband amidst the fresh wave of chaos.

Civilians left and right were flocking towards one of the most southernmost cities on the peninsula, Busan, in order to escape the invasion from the north. Women and children were given car rides, while men took trains. A family friend of Mr. Kim, who was in the army, provided transportation for Mrs. Hur and her children. Along the way, the car flipped around, leaving everyone inside scathed, but they sought medical help at the military infirmary as soon as they arrived in Busan. Mrs. Hur soon met up with Mr. Kim once again.

The overall story of Mrs. Hur and Mr. Kim is one of true love and always finding each other after times of hardship. No matter what, they sought to reunite with each other. And though the couple found happiness in Seoul after the Korean War ended, it lasted for only a few decades. Due to complications in his liver, Mr. Kim passed away in 1985, leaving Mrs. Hur widowed and alone in witnessing the growth of her children's children. Of all the few memories I have of spending time with my great-grandmother, many are of how she always gazed at her husband's medals hanging on the walls. She looked upon them with great admiration and affection, and was always willing to share stories about him. The kind of love she once had for her husband is, and will always be, something for me to look up to.

Times were extremely hard in Busan. Mrs. Hur's family was all together now, but they were cramped in tiny rooms shared with several other refugees. New floods of fugitives came in every single week, crowding up each infirmary and hospital. Not only was the space small, but food was scarce as well. Luckily, Mr. Kim landed a job as an English translator for the Americans helping out around the area. His position was envied by many, as earning any sort of salary was all a game of fortune, and it gave the family a reliant source of money.

Things got better whenever soldiers came around to distribute leftover flour. Mrs. Hur would put all of the flour dough into a big pot of soup and boil it, giving out bowls to each person. But it was never enough. Everyone was left with hunger in their stomachs. Mrs. Hur's children wouldn't let go of their spoons after finishing their bowl because they were still so hungry. Even when she scoured the hills outside for grass to put into the soup, it was never enough. Every meal was measly and limited.

This helps me understand why finishing a meal is such an integral part of dinner propriety in my family. Even when the leftover foods on my plate are all foods I don't want to eat—this happens more times then I would like to admit—my mom scolds me and tells me that unless I finish every single crumb, I am not allowed to get up from the table. At first, this was a mere annoyance in my daily meals, but now I am beginning to understand my mother's reasons. Had my great-grandmother been alongside me in every dinner I ever ate, she would have gone pale at how much I take everything for granted. She would have finished her meal with prim table manners while I remained picking at the food with my fork. Another point to highlight the disparity between generations of different centuries.

Years passed as war raged on, and Mrs. Hur spent days rubbing her children's stomachs and comforting them to sleep, as well as doing her best to provide room, food, and comfort for everyone else around her. Mr. Kim worked endlessly to provide for them. While the United States was always there to help the south, times were still extremely difficult.

The Korean War halted in 1953. An armistice was signed by both sides of the war—with representatives from both halves of the Korean population and their respective allies—to start a temporal ceasefire. The DMZ was created to split the peninsula at 38 degrees of latitude, effectively creating a partition, and war prisoners were warily exchanged. But even though the bloodshed had been toned down, a formal treaty was never signed. The Korean War has not officially been deemed over, and tension still surrounds the north and the south. It is unknown how long this precarious peace will last.

When I was growing up in Korea as a young child, my school used to host annual trips to North Korea to donate food and necessities to people suffering from tuberculosis. Back then, I thought nothing much of it—we were being charitable and helping people in need. But now, I realize the significance of this. Not only were we, as South Koreans, comfortably traveling between both halves of the peninsula, but we were helping out people in North Korea. I have not been raised to particularly despise the people living north, nor have I been raised to treat them as equals or allies, but this memory gives me hope that maybe, despite all the tension surrounding it and the rest of the world, the tranquility reigning between both sides is more stable than I have thought it to be. Or perhaps this is not true, and things are more dangerous than ever. But whatever the case, I am glad that there was some sort of harmonious interaction between the north and the south, with the country my great-grandmother once called home.

After the Korean War informally ended, Mrs. Hur went back to Seoul with her husband and two children to start her life again. Mr. Kim enlisted in the Air Force as an officer, and later got appointed by the president himself as a minister and ambassador. These two roles earned him the myriad of medals now hanging on my great-grandmother's walls. The remainder of the children's youths flew by with relative ease. It seemed that the dust had now settled.

Though everything was significantly better, a new country had emerged broken and trampled. Everyone was grieving for what had been lost during years of suffering. An entire nation was laying in wait to be repaired, supporting masses of people marked with wounds and scars. The end of a bloody era had been reached, and it marked the start of the next age—one filled with new beginnings.

Today, Mrs. Hur lies not in her house gazing wistfully up at her husband's medals of honor, but in a casket that was lowered into the ground mere weeks ago.

She was 98 at the time of her passing. Her last years were spent largely in the hospital, facing obstacle after obstacle, only to overcome each one with a resilience deemed miraculous by her doctors. But for the past few months, her sickness was a tumultuous journey that kept her confined in the hospital, with nobody knowing how long it would last. It lasted until December 17, 2023, when it is said her pain was eased away to give her a peaceful death.

Mrs. Hur will always be remembered for her courage as a young woman fleeing from North Korea. She will always be remembered as the anchor of what our family has become today, flourishing and successful, as it is all in thanks to her that our life may be this privileged. She will always be remembered as a figure of incredibly admirable strength.

My name is Becky Lee. I am the great-granddaughter of Mrs. Hur, and I am proud to be her descendant.

It is my burden to live with the memory of her sacrifices and the weight of her legacy.

It is my honor to carve my story into stone, just as she once did.

Eliot Jones was born completely colorblind.

Nobody knew how it had happened. Neither his mother nor his father had any sort of sight impairment, and nothing affected his grandparents, uncles and aunts, and cousins, either. He opened his eyes to the world seeing nothing but black, white, and gray.

His mother had always been a lovely shade of pearl-gray, with stiff, straight hair like a cloud. His father, on the other hand, had skin like it was meant to blend into the shadows. He had a broad nose and curly black hair.

Eliot liked seeing them kiss. He liked seeing them hold hands and touch foreheads and hug each other. But they never did it outside the house. He could remember one instance when they did, when he was seven years old. They were eating out at the town's favorite Italian diner. His parents always ate on opposite sides of the table, with Eliot somewhere in the middle. Usually they never touched. But that day it was their tenth wedding anniversary, and they kissed when the cake came out.

"Mister, missus, please refrain from doing that in public," the waiter had said somewhat awkwardly.

An old lady at the next table over tsked. "And in front of your own child, too! Heavens!"

Later, while his father was signing the bill so they could go back home, Eliot spotted a couple sitting in the back. They both had pearl skin and cloud hair just like his mother. When the waiter gave them their bread, they kissed sweetly over the table, but nobody said anything.

There was never another incident quite like that—at least, not one that Eliot could remember. He grew up in a childhood that could not be described as turbulent. At school, all of his classmates' skins were more like his father's, not his mother's. His teachers', too. But at home, their neighborhood housed people like his mother. Sometimes, the only thing that let Eliot distinguish between all the neighborhood mothers from his own were their unique facial features and the colors of their hair.

One neighborhood mother that Eliot saw a lot was Mrs. Miller, who lived next door. She had pearly skin, just like his mother, but her hair was almost as black as his father's. Whenever she walked over to visit, Eliot would greet her very politely, just as instructed by his mother. But Mrs. Miller would only pat his cheek once and then move on to greet his mother. His mother didn't seem to mind. They would always sit on the two armchairs near the unused fireplace and talk in hushed whispers, nursing small cups of tea in their dainty little saucers. Mrs. Miller was never here when Eliot's father came back from work.

It was a sunny spring day in Eliot's twelfth year when his father came back home early from work while Mrs. Miller was still with his mother. Eliot was sitting at the kitchen doing his arithmetics, which he had been struggling with for awhile in school. His arithmetics teacher, Mr. Garcia, told all of his students that perfection came with practice.

When the sound of his father's Volkswagen Beetle grew louder, Eliot peered out the window and saw the near-white car pulling into the driveway. His father stepped out and whistled as he neared the front porch, jangling his keys all the way up the walkway. The hushed whispers of Eliot's mother and Mrs. Miller grew silent altogether.

When the front door opened, Eliot jumped to his feet as always and ran up to greet his father. His father, like always, ruffled Eliot's hair and patted his head. "My boy!" he said, like always. "How are you, my boy?"

Eliot, like always, said he was doing well. His father didn't like it when he said *good*. *Good* was never an answer to *How are you* and it drove his father crazy sometimes.

His father, like always, took off his coat and hung it neatly above his polished oxford shoes. He took his briefcase and put it on the side table next to his keys, like always. Then he walked into the sitting room and saw Mrs. Miller sitting rather rigidly in her armchair to the right of the fireplace. His father also became rather rigid.

Eliot's mother jumped to her feet and smoothed the wrinkles of her skirt. "You're back earlier than usual! I don't know if you remember Maeve. She and her husband Tom live next door. Their daughters are already off to college! I don't know if you remember. This is Maeve."

His mother was blabbering, just slightly. She always blabbered slightly whenever she was nervous.

His father, ever the gentleman, straightened his tie and outstretched a hand. "Pleasure to meet you, Mrs. Maeve."

Mrs. Miller took the hand of Eliot's father and shook it, just once. Then she dropped it quickly and hid her hands behind her back. Eliot wondered if he was the only one to notice the small wrinkle that had found its way into Mrs. Miller's narrow nose.

"The pleasure is mine, Mr. Jones," Mrs. Miller said back. "You have a lovely house."

Mr. Jones guffawed loudly. Eliot was old enough to know that it was his tactic to ease tension. "Why, I've never heard that before! Thank you. Though I've driven by your house enough times to know that your lawn is more manicured than mine could ever be."

Mrs. Miller observed his father with shrewd eyes. She had always had really shrewd eyes. "Pray tell, with whose money was this house bought? Yours, or your wife's? I've heard that her father was born into a family of high class."

Eliot was old enough to know that the pause that followed was very tense.

He expected his father to guffaw again. Instead of guffawing, he looked at Mrs. Miller very carefully, and opened his mouth to speak.

"Eliot," his mother butted in quickly, "why don't you finish your homework in your room? Dinner will be in an hour."

Eliot wanted to argue, but knew better to in the company of Mrs. Miller. So he took his bag and his papers and went to his room. He shut his door and finished his homework, his arithmetics that would lead to perfection, in Mr. Garcia's words.

When he came back out for dinner, his father was in the master bedroom with the door closed. His mother stood at the stove alone, stirring tomato soup with her apron on. She beckoned Eliot towards the dining table without words and served him a full bowl.

The next day when his father came back from work, he didn't ask Eliot how he was doing. He didn't call him *my boy*. He went straight to the master bedroom and shut the door again. When the time for dinner came, the door remained closed, and no words were spoken.

As time passed, Eliot slowly noticed bags piling up along the wall outside the master bedroom. Every day, his father came back home from work, and would then go straight to his room and close the door. Still, not a word was said between the two. Mrs. Miller even stopped visiting. His mother sat alone in the armchair to the left of the fireplace every day and would read or sew. With every day that passed, Eliot did his arithmetic homework. His numbers got more and more perfect, and Mr. Garcia got prouder and prouder.

Eliot came back from school on his thirteenth birthday, twenty-seven days later after Mrs. Miller's last visit, to see the bags that had been slowly accumulating were completely gone. The door to the master bedroom was still closed. Mrs. Miller was nowhere to be seen. His mother was not sitting on her armchair reading nor sewing. Eliot, not knowing what to do or what to say, went to his bedroom and did his arithmetic homework.

When he came back out for dinner, his mother was wearing her apron, standing at the stove and stirring garlic soup. She beckoned Eliot towards the dining table without words and served him a full bowl.

Finally, as Eliot picked up his cold, cold spoon, he opened his mouth and asked, "Where's father?

His mother, with her pearl skin and cloud hair, looked into his eyes with her dull gray ones and said, "Gone."

The following evening, Eliot completed his arithmetic homework in his bedroom. It wasn't as difficult as it used to be, but he was still struggling with division. He saw the little symbol on the white sheet, and saw nothing but two faces divided.

Mrs. Miller was back near the fireplace that day, on the right side, talking to his mother in whispers less hushed than before. When dinner came an hour later, Eliot left his room and ate with his mother and Mrs. Miller.

POEMS

how does it feel to be trapped in one body? two worlds separated

by flesh and soul, ruling their own domains. so much overlaps

that sometimes i can't tell the difference between them, yet

sometimes i can't help but gape at the contrast. here, where

my flesh stands out, i embrace my soul. i dig my feet into the

other world like i truly belong, like i cannot possibly be anything—

anything but the paragon of perfect patriotism. but there, where

my flesh doesn't stand out, the other world shuns me because i

am nothing but a stranger donning the wrong mask, the wrong

color. soul invades flesh. white bleeds into yellow, and i am lost

trying to find my way to the other world without a map or compass.

on the winding journey, i stumble upon the crossroads where i see

a chance, a world; a staple binding the unknown and the familiar.

FOOTPRINTS

There I walk alone

following the tracks   that

           lead north,

dusted with snow.

Nothing ever looked   lonelier

           or older.

In the distance,

the call of a horn   slips

           through

the fog's wall.

I look down at   the

           pure white.

On the other side,

following the tracks,   is a

           silhouette;

blanketed by mist,

silent in the snow,   without

           footprints.

I call out to it,

like a bellow   from the

          belly of

the monster that

runs across with   furious

          speed.

An apparition,

it turns back to   glance

          at me.

Its smile is the

only thing I see   as I

          beckon.

With doe-light feet

that make no   crunch

          over snow,

the ghost dances,

crossing over   to

                                         me.

Its taloned feet

slipping over the   frozen

                                         tracks,

a monster runs,

baring its teeth,   opening

                                         its claws,

barreling into the

misty figure.   The smile

                                         is gone.

I see nothing now.

No blood or bones,   and no

                                         footprints.

The monster flies,

its maws now closed,

I cannot help but

smile back at it,

Out from the snow

appears a body.

along the tracks,

leaving not a hint

of our footprints.

       eyes glinting

          at me.

       and then

          it's gone.

       We dance

          together

YOUR LITTLE DOLL

You glance down at me with eyes

That are wide and full of scrutiny

Go ahead, have a poke at my skin

Touch my hair, inspect my body

You see that little blemish on my face

And it ignites a little fire inside you

You come back again and it's gone

I can never say a single word

When you twist my arms and legs

When you bend my fingers back

When you drop me on the floor

When you pull out my strands

When you gouge at my eyes

My mouth is fixed in the same shape

You pinch at my cheeks scornfully

Deem my skin too yellow or too wan

Tsk at the gray bags under my eyes

Correct my posture as I sit on my chair

And watch, like a hawk, everything that

Goes into my mouth, down my throat

Everything that goes on my skin, or

When the moon lulls or the sun rouses me

Or how my body bends as I rest

And the days when you tire from me

I sit in my little dollhouse all day long

My altered face fixed with a smile

Back ramrod-straight, hands in my lap

Staring at the clock as it ticks, tocks

Collecting dust in my aging hair

Until you come back and brush it out

My limbs move like those of a marionette

I sip tea like a prim, posh princess

I read books etched with fancy ink

I sit alone at oak dining tables for feasts

Well, isn't this everyone's dream life

I yield as you make me dance around

And at night when you continue to dream

I sit stiffly on my shelf and watch you

When the fog gets to me, I fall over

You wake up and spot me and scold me

Harshly push my body upright again
The dollhouse windows flutter with my sigh
But there is nothing else that I can do
My arms are fixed out towards you
Always reaching for your touch
My eyes are always wide and unblinking
Waiting to see what happens next

This is the only life I have ever known
I remain in this corner of your room
While you grow taller and taller and
Eventually hand me down to your child
I watch dutifully, with immortal eyes,
As everything happens all over again
And I can never say a single word

DUPLEX (PAPER IN A RAINSTORM)

The first time he left for Korea, I cried
Which is strange to think about now

      What's strange to think about is that now
      I barely blink when he leaves

I barely blink when he grieves
About the sweetheart I once was

      I was once such a sweetheart
      Giving his sandpaper stubble kisses

Giving his sandpaper stubble kisses
All flies away, a paper in a rainstorm

      A paper in a rainstorm, I fly away
      A peck to the cheek, a quick hug is all now

A peck to the cheek, a quick hug was all
The first time he left for Korea, I cried

SUNSET & SHADOW

I. Sunset

Saturday, December 16, 2023

The sunset today isn't anything extraordinary
Just the usual swash of yellow, orange and blue
My mom and I sit in the car listening to the radio
Driving home, driving towards the sinking sun
Laughing and smiling together with festive cheer
I sing along to Ariana Grande and her perfect voice
Before the phone rings ominously, cutting us off

It's grandfather, I tell her, and she answers the call
A frantic rush of Korean, words I barely understand
But I pick up enough, even from Mom's gasps and sighs
It's her grandmother, the heart of our entire family
Helpless on a hospital bed and moments from death
The doctors are calling in all family—an emergency
I stay silent and keep my eyes on the dying horizon

The radio has been made noiseless at some point

I don't feel like singing along to carols anymore
The call ends, and Mom drives in complete silence
The only thing my miserable mind can muster is: *oh, no*
Calls are made to more family members of the news
My aunt laments into the phone: *oh, boyyyyyy*
And I keep on sitting there silently, looking at all
The silhouettes against the backdrop of the sunset
Some walking left, some walking right, and the sky,
I think to myself—it has never looked more beautiful

We get home in the rays of the sun's reaching hands
And descend into the garage under the newly indigo sky
Mom doesn't know what to do—a week before Christmas,
And suddenly everything is interrupted by one phone call
She smiles reassuringly but it's dimmed in the sun's absence
Here I sit in my room now, tapping away on a computer
—because what else is there that I can do? Nothing?—
While my mom grieves over the phone and whispers
Again and again, very quietly, like I can't hear, my name

The truth is, I don't even know my great-grandmother well
When I think of her, I think of frail bones and wrinkly skin
Immobile in a wheelchair—it's terrible, I know, but

My life goes on without her, without thoughts of her

Except during times like these when I become just an

Anchor rooting my mom down in my harbor, when

All she wants to do is sail back home to her grandmother

Maybe the only thing keeping her here are my knots

Firmly mooring her to my dilapidated wooden deck

But I sit back on my beach and gaze up, thinking

Nothing ever looked more beautiful than the sunset,

And the night sky tonight, with all of its sparkling city lights.

II. Shadow

Sunday, December 17, 2023

The next day, in the devil's hour, the dreaded message arrives

Here in America, everything happened in two different days

But there in Korea, it all happened over the course of one

Called into the hospital at dawn, witnessing death at dusk

And it seems so, so, so unfair now that I look back at it

That the doctors could tell us, one morning, that she's fine

But then later that same day it turns out to all be a trick?

My great-grandmother had been hospitalized for awhile

It was a jump-scare at first, but we'd gotten used to it

'Til that famous call and we all worried ourselves to sleep
No more overcoming medical jump-scares now; she's gone

My mom came barrelling into my room at 8 AM today
Dressed in her pajamas, hair askew, tired eyes and all
With the news from Korea that her grandmother just died
I didn't cry, and neither did she, what a strong woman
Calm in her troubles to remedy her annihilated plans
Until she left, closed the door, let me go back to sleep
And I was left lying in the shadows of my bedroom
Tears leaking from my eyes to stain the pillow and blanket
Stifling my sniffles in the soft fur of my sleeping dog
Why do I cry? Out of true sorrow for a lost beloved one?
Or some knee-jerk reaction to the death of someone I know?

It's not until after Mom leaves when memories come back
Bowing to the floor in front of the dignified figure that is her
Seeing her try on new clothes and scarves and laugh in joy
Serving us ice cream and yogurts as our favorite treats
Sitting at the center, quietly looking on in family reunions
Clasping my hand and telling me I'm a beautiful girl
Wistfully looking over all of her husband's medals
Hunched over permanently but with a loud, strong voice

Waving us farewell from her wheelchair in the veranda

All of them will, and always be, my great-grandmother

The tears have stopped falling now, though the sniffles remain

I'm sitting on my disheveled bed, computer in my lap, writing

With an aching back, sticky cheeks, and swollen little eyes

I cannot find it in myself to stand, get out of bed, leave the room

The day has started all around me, and it has for Mom, too

But I can't; I'll just stay here in the dim confines of my room

Typing away on a computer like I've always been doing

Reminiscing in the shadows, hiding from the morning

Thinking of her.

EIGHT SILVER GEESE

Eight silver geese all fly as one

Towards the flickering beacon at home

Wings stretched out for those grasping frail hands

Wailing sad lullabies as they fly

The whole world stops to see them pass by

Swooping delicately over cold lands

Keeping formation like all geese who roam

Two of them gray, six of them young

My mama happens to be one of them

A goose flying far in the harsh winter airs

Everything suddenly abandoned to pause

She left after the beacon's call, at night

All of the geese spread wing and took flight

Now a ~~white~~ black Christmas, no Santa Claus

But I'll anyway to the sky give my prayers

And then open gifts slowly, lonesome

Well, where is a small silver gosling to stay?

Our nest is now empty of food and of warmth

A gentle white wing gives me cover and shield

Cooing gently as the twigs fall apart

Rest in peace, loved one, you'll be in our hearts

Except it's hard to believe when it's all so surreal

This goose has made many journeys from birth

Now we'll see her soul off and away

Legends of the honorable gray-feathered goose

Migrated from north to south early on

Lived through a war of violence and blood

Laid three golden eggs, witnessed one's death

Watched as her mate took his very last breath

Built her new nest up from the mud

Taught the flight basics to the third generation

After this much hard work, nature's letting her loose

One goose has been flying since the breakout of dawn

One goose flies north, interrupting his vacation

One goose leaves his old, weathered nest

One goose gets out of his job to fly alone

One goose leaves her two little eggs back at home

One goose flies home to the beacon from the west

One goose flies from the other end of the nation

One goose, the last goose—I told you, she's gone

And so they flock on to the beacon of light

Flying to see her eyes forever closed

Flying to see her body laid to rest

Flying to bless her journey to heaven

To thank her for all of the joy she's given

To lay her down in the capsule of death

Flying while the universe has frozen

They fly without stop, all through the night

Isn't this honorable gray-feathered goose our creator?

We are all silver; not white, not brown

Our feathers are spun from threads of the moon

We live in the comforting shade of her wing

There is a reason we do not honk, we sing

It's a tragedy she had to leave us so soon

She's responsible for the life I know now

And for that I will always be grateful to her

This gray-feathered goose was nearly a century

Snatched away by nature before the time came

Three days of farewell 'til the ground eats her whole

Eight geese follow her down all the way

The rest of us descendants in tow behind

There she'll find peace, peace there to stay

Alone 'til the next beacon flickers and falls

No honorable gray-feathered goose is the same

For she is the first silver goose of our history

REBECCA SERIM LEE

Rebecca Serim Lee is currently a ninth grader at Noble and Greenough School. She has enjoyed writing from a very young age and wrote stories throughout her elementary and middle school years. Her other hobbies include playing the piano and clarinet, as well as spending time with family, friends, and her dog. She has recently taken up filmmaking as a new interest. Rebecca's favorite genres to read about are fantasy fiction and Dystopian fiction. Her favorite genres to write in are poetry, short stories in realistic or science fiction, and personal essay/memoir. She loves to write about her family and important memories, as well as anything else that pops up in her mind. Rebecca reads and writes for fun and enjoys submitting her works to competitions and sharing them with others.